OGMIOS
RISING
The Book of Ogmios:
Book 1
JP RALEY

Ogmios Rising

(The Book of Ogmios: Book 1)

JP Raley

Cover design: JP Raley

First edition, 2022

Part 1 in the book series: The Book of Ogmios

ISBN: 9798839094253

Ogmios Rising

The Book of Ogmios: Book 1

For my Giessen and South Garland Families

And to those who believed in and supported my dreams

Chapter 1

Darkness. An echoing knock on a wooden door repeats three times the same. Silence. Three more times, an echoing knock on a wooden door repeats in the same manner. Silence. An echoing knock on a wooden door begins its third repetitive start, only to be interrupted after the next first try when the creaking sound of the wooden door is heard before the second knock can be made. Then, silence once more. That is until footsteps can be heard shuffling through the darkness and the creaking sound of a wooden door being closed.

Then, the sound of a match being struck against its home is heard as the faint glow of the match's reason for existing slowly brightens to full life. The match then moves through the air as though it were dancing a lonesome, slow Walz, being mindful of each step it takes in tune with the sound of unsee shuffling fee. The match's slow dance continues on for a bit more until it remains still before it rises as though it were about to give a toast to its once meaningful life. Then, the outline of a lantern is seen with a candle inside as the match lays down its life so that the candle can begin its own, and the lantern's latch is closed so as to protect it.

The lantern then is carefully raised until the face of an older man is seen trying to make the acquaintance between the darkness, his eyes, and the candle's light. The old man slowly walks forward through the darkness before him, occasionally looking down toward his feet as though the candlelight was telling him to be careful with each step. Through the mixture of the light's shadows gently nudging away the darknesses' hold, the older man takes note of the room he's now standing in.

Looking around, the man sees a room in shambles, old pieces of furniture covered in blankets of dust with old books and unseen faces of pictures littering an old wooden floor as though it were part of a snowglobe shaken up.

Winter's breath grees the man's life as he lifts the lantern a little higher until the squint of his eye reveals what he wants to see as he begins to talk a bit furthermore. The old man is now standing before what appears to be a long hallway, and as his eyes adjust, he sees the outline of multiple doorways on each side of the corridor that has an ever more darkened end.

Then, an unseen voice calls out, "Well, aren't you going to open one of them up?". The man responds, "Ain't you gonna tell me which one?". "Where would the fun be in that?" the unseen voice responds back. After looking around, the man closes his eyes for a few moments before reopening them. Then, he stretches out his hand to the door before him, turns the knob, then opens it. More darkness greets him. "Well," the old man says out loud, "Here goes nothing" as he steps into the darkness before him as the door closes behind him under its own power.

The man holds up his lantern as he looks around and sees nothing. "What is this place?" the man thinks out loud. Silence responds back with not a sound being given. Then, the sound of a heartbeat is heard as though it were coming from all around him. "This," an unseen voice says to the old man, "This is the moment where your life begins." The man's eyes begin to give a look of desperation as he knows that he is no longer alone as a shadowy figure emerges its head over the man's right shoulder to where the man now stands, frozen as it does. Without a seen mouth, the dark mist says, "Let's take this from the beginning, shall we?" as it blows out the old man's candle, leaving both him and the shadow in complete darkness once more.

Chapter 2

Dreams and placement, nine months of preparation and purpose. A baby is born alive and healthy, just as how most other human babies come into a fallen world. A pair of newborn blue eyes open briefly to a new yet quite familiar sight before the baby's eyes close gently once more as a smile that only a newborn can give across its mouth. Proud parents in a hospital recovery room, holding the gently sleeping baby with a helpful nurse nearby, and additional visiting family members in the room.

The newborn baby sees with a fuzzy observation for a brief moment while reopening its eyes. As expected, the newborn begins to figure out its mother and father by turning its attention to the sounds it hears. Every voice and smile begets even more smiles just to capture the little angel's heavenly gaze. As expected, the newborn baby turns its attention to the voice of the moment.

These natural interactions continue for a bit longer, but in a quick moment, something draws the baby's attention away as though someone new came into the room. Instinctively, as though directed to do so, everyone's heads turn toward the direction that the newborn's head had been fixated on. As expected, no one is seen. All eyes move slightly over to the closed door, half expecting someone to enter the room, but no one ever does. So, thinking that the newborn angel is just trying to adjust to the new world, everyone refixed all their love back toward the once more sleepy newborn.

As the new eyes begin to close their precious sight for a nap, the darling angel again fixes its gaze on a part of unseen shadows discreetly hidden behind everyone else in the room that only the newborn can see. Dreams once more embrace the newborn baby with sweet sounds of placement, purpose, and design.

As the newborn baby begins to nap once more, the two unseen shadows still stand silent as it seems the shadowy pair are observing the room's activities. Then, one of the shadows begins to form the familiar form of the old man while the other remains as is. With a slight crackling sound to its voice as it begins to speak, the shadow says to the old man, "This is the day that you were born into the world. There are reasons you may not recall, but you were created for a purpose". "To what? Asked the old man, who is now fully visible yet still unseen to the others who are still looking at both the newborn and newly crowned mother.

"That is something only The Creator knows," the shadow replies, "Something for us all to discover ourselves. Sometimes with help, sometimes not. Come, let me see what we remember else", the shadow says as it concludes its brief message. Reaching out to the old man with what should be an arm, the old man begins to change into a shadowy mist as the two slowly dissipate in the same manner as they came.

Shards of darkness and light begin to flash across the old man's eyes as he sees his life from the moment he remembers alongside memories being recalled through those shards. The man then sees his memories as a two-year-old, remembering when his mother was pregnant with his sister, the birth of his younger cousins, and the world's events ranging from Nixon to Carter with wars, crises, losses, and celebrations all in between. The shards also continue to show the man's memories as happiness comes to his smile as he sees his father, lost relatives, and Christmases that stir his emotions.

Then, as the shards of dark and light begin to slow in intensity, the old man sees the days he began school through the early second grade before total darkness once more embraces his eyes. Then, the sound of a creaking door is heard as the candle in the old man's lantern once more comes back to life, beckoning him to step back through the door in which he first entered. Once through, the man slowly shuffles a bit back more in the hallway as he watches the door slowly creaking shut as it fades away as though it never was there at all.

Then, a familiar unseen voice speaks again, "Well? What are you waiting for?". The old man carefully maneuvers his lantern as he turns with it as he tries to get his eyes readjusted between the candle's light and the darkness as he looks down the hallway at the remaining six doors. Faintly, the old man says, "I'm tired of making the wrong choices, and when I think I make the right one, I get hurt in some way. If this is some sort of trip down memory lane, well, all my memories are long gone. I've loved and lived, sometimes thinking I could've done better, but needless to say, I will not play your games. I came here searching for something while trying to get out of winter's cold embrace, but I can't remember why I was drawn to this house, to begin with".

A singular low growl begins to be heard after the old man speaks that echoes through the hallway's walls for a few moments that seem like forever before silence takes over once more. Then, one of the other doors can be heard in the darkness slowly creaking open with unseen footsteps now being heard approaching the old man. A young girl's voice then calls out, What's the matter, Jay? Don't want to play games with me?" just as she slowly walks out of a now opened door.

The old man raises the lantern slightly so that he can get a better look at the young girl, and as he does, his eyes open up in disbelief. "It can't be," the man whispers out loud. "Did you think that your journey in existence was a solitary one? Did you not care to think that it was not your own decision that was at stake?" the girl starts to scream as she lifts her right arm upwards, lifting the old man as she does. "Do you think life is a game, Jay? Yes, you may have the ability to see and travel the life cycles, but it wasn't just your decision alone to make!", as the girl's last words turn to loud growls as she flings both her arms and the old man towards the second open door, with the old man disappearing into the darkness and the door slamming shut behind him.

The girl stands alone, eyes reflecting the darkness that continues to surround her as she relentlessly stares at the door through which she just flung the old man through. Through a nearby window behind her, the moon briefly shines a solitary beam of light that passes through the girl and onto the floor below her that also briefly shines its life so that a solitary tear can be seen falling from her eyes as they turn alive with color before the tear hits the old wooden floor. As clouds pass in front of the moon's light, the girl says out loud as though she had an audience listening to her, "We need you to remember, Jay, so that we may all continue to live. I need you to remember, Jay" as

her last words dissipate just as she does with the last gleam

of moonlight before silent darkness returns once more.

Chapter 3

Seven sides with each a voice of reason of their own accord. Think of them as a variation of the five senses that a typical human controls. However, for Jay, these additional seven variances each represent an extra layer of support within his life. A sixth sense for his unconscious mind making connections between seemingly unrelated events, so to speak. Jay uses these variations on top of his natural birth skills of being an INTJ and a Scorpio that utilizes his whole-brained analysis to help him navigate his life between the known and the unknown.

The darkness that Jay now finds himself in has his thoughts repeating the same voices of variation over and over through his head as he falls through nothingness. Seeing that girl triggered a long-lost memory within Jay's memory, and that image of her repeats in opposite cycles while the repeatable words cycle over and over again. Then, a new set of memories seemingly open a new path of remembrance, as Jay recalls when he was a baby in a crib, where life's mysteries began with the invisible making its presence known.

Jay recalls the times in which a bedroom closet door would open and close under its own power or when the flicking of a light switch would amuse him rather than frighten him. Other times Jay would see his bedroom door crack open a bit more, and rather than seeing his mom or dad peeking in on him, Jay would see nothing instead. Or, even yet, Jay would catch glimpses of shadows moving at the corner of his eye that would continue to follow him well to this very day. While these events did not bother Jay growing up, his thirst for the unknown would only intensify even further for him over the years.

Looking back over his life, Jay thinks about what he has seen, what he thought he knew and thinks about the roads not taken. Jay realizes that there were moments when time stood still and unknowingly knew that he had to make a life-altering decision. What Jay didn't know at those moments were the subjects of what and how to which decisions were being needed to be taken. Life is about living and living in the moment, so why does Jay still feel so conflicted?

Looking back, it still seems like Jay has lived his memories as though he had only lived them just a few months ago. However, the last time Jay remembers looking into a mirror, time reminds him that it was actually more than just a few months ago and as to why it was hard for him to wrap his mind around the actual concept of the present time.

Jay's thoughts then turn to relatives that he has spent time with, places that both he and his sister went to together with their parents, the friends he had made back in school, along with the personal and professional relationships that he has forged and have lost over the same span of time. Jay's thoughts continue to look a bit closer to his personal relationships, especially the girls he wanted and the wives he had and lost. Going even further, Jay's thoughts begin to recall the actual madness of those enduring years, especially during high school, where it was as though a type of madness would emerge that allowed him to see the what-ifs of each person that continued well into adulthood.

Did Jay truly ever understand the depths of love? Jay naturally shrugs off those negative thoughts because, yes, while he did indeed understand the depths of love, the problem was actually that he didn't remain focused on just one love. Instead, Jay realizes even further that he let the different paths of possibilities and what-ifs distract him from being focused in the here and now on just one person. Continuing to recall his past memories, Jay easily sees where those moments of critical decision-making came into play and where the branches of those decisions actually lived on whether or not Jay had indeed taken them. Jay's thoughts then turn around back to the present moment of what feels like an endless fall into nothingness in the here and now.

Jay's thoughts turn him to dwell more deeply on the face of the little girl and her words of condemnation for his actions when he was but a younger man in high school. Even though total darkness engulfs Jay from every side, and despite the sensation of him falling, Jay's memories cannot help but think of the very first time that he met the girl named Cherise, the very same girl that Jay just saw before throwing him through an open dark doorway. Then, Jay feels as though his descent is slowing down dramatically as though an invisible parachute had just been opened, causing Jay's body to straighten up more as though he were preparing to land on an unseen piece of earth.

How can his thoughts be out of sync with time? Was it a naturally occurring degradation of his body that has caused so much unbalance in his life? Was it because of some retribution for not following the rules he had set up in agreement with God and declaring his current lifecycle as a sabbatical cycle of observation? Jay's mind thinks of his image of a now old but once young man as he debates his own mind's shards of coexistence and wonders how he could have been so careless of how each lifecycle should have been touched differently. Then, the darkness that surrounded Jay now begins to show a trace of life as light seemingly begins to be slowly introduced until his eyes set upon a memory of when he was eight years old.

Jay's memories, and his thoughts, all collide on the girl who had thrown him through the door versus the actual girl Jay remembers as an eight-year-old kid. The memories Jay has of this little girl take him back to when he first met Cherise at a daycare where both his and Cherise's parents would drop them off in the morning time. It still seems like it was not long ago when Jay recalls looking around the center and seeing this young girl playing at a tiny version of a kitchen by herself, pretending to be cooking. "Whatcha doing?" Jay recalls asking the young girl as he shyly approached her. "Playing house," the young girl responded and then asked, "Want to help me by cooking? Here, stir this pot while I put something in the oven. Oh, and by the way, I'm Cherise". "Hi, Cherise," Jay responded back, "I'm Jay. And, yes, I'd love to help you cook and play house with you!".

Jay's memories then continue to focus on his and Cherise's interactions over the weeks that turned into months as Jay and Cherise would find themselves sharing the same class in the first half of the second grade. It seemed as though these two kids were inseparable. Then, an event took place that would change how often Jay and Cherise would see one another. As Jay's father was in the Army and had already been transferred to West Germany, the notice came in via Jay's mother that he, his mom, and his younger sister would all be joining Jay's dad in Europe.

Naturally, Jay's mom notified the elementary school that he and his sister would be leaving, but what came next would help continue the connection between Jay and Cherise as their shared class would see the teacher having each of the students write to Jay as a pen pal exchange. While these moments still live with Jay as an important part of his life, they would not be the striking point that would be attached to his soul's understanding of the world around him. No, it would be along the way that would begin the continuation of Jay's ability to comprehend his world.

Jay's memories then turn to the moments in which he would gain an earache along the way to West Germany, which would cause him to begin not feeling good. Upon landing, Jay would deal with the earache as best he could and be happy to see his father again while absorbing the beautiful new scenery around him. Jay's memories become choppy at this point because of this detail, but the next showing would remind Jay of so many things that he did not know at the time.

Jay's memories then see him waking up from a nap that seemed like an eternal slumber. Jay sees himself slowly opening up his eyes while they take their time to adjust to a darkened room. However, that darkened room was backlit by the open kitchen's location to where Jay saw his mother cooking dinner. "Hey, sleepyhead," Jay's mother said, "I was wondering when you were going to wake up." Before Jay even gives a response, his thoughts still reverberate through time and are part of the definition of what Jay now understands as he watches himself through time.

Jay recalls his thoughts telling him that it was good to see his mother again and knew that his father was still alive. "Where's dad?" Jay would first ask his mom. "Oh, he went out to go get some medicine for you on base and should be back at any moment," his mother would reply. At the time, Jay would not understand why these thoughts and moments would remain with him specifically, but looking back, it all makes sense as the darkness began to creep back in around Jay as his descent would begin anew.

The voice of the girl that had thrown Jay through the darkened door is now heard, telling Jay that there are moments when decisions taken and actions not taken would define everything Jay would ever come to know. Flashes of moments cross Jay's descent through the darkness as he would see the lightning bolt of when he would go out and have his arm and shoulder broken as one such moment that defined him. However, the girl's voice would then also remind Jay that an even bigger quake was about to come across his and others' lives that was still to come to pass.

Then, Jay's descent once more comes to a slow halt as the girl's voice continues to say that this was about to be the moment that would define not only his life but the young woman's life as well as the girl's voice began to shift toward an older teenager's voice. "This," the young woman's voice continued, "This is the moment that you decided that you wanted a sabbatical lifecycle to see beyond what you already had known. This was the moment where an eternity of lines would be forged that would see Jay continuously traveling until he once more found the right one on which to travel.

The young woman then speaks again, saying, "You do remember this moment, don't you?" while light begins to engulf Jay as he sees his younger self walking through busy school hallways until he walks past the school's cafeteria where he stops to look at. Jay sees himself looking down at his watch and then looking back into the cafeteria as though he were looking for someone until he does. Then, Jay walks into the cafeteria until he stands before a young teenage woman. As Jay looks upon himself looking at this scene, the older Jay turns his head away as though he wants to avoid seeing a heartbreak being relived over and over again.

"No!" screams the woman's voice from the darkness, still being held back behind the older Jay's back. "You will look, and you will remember!" yells the woman while a shadowy hand forces Jay's head to look once more at his younger self standing before the young woman in the school's cafeteria. As the older Jay is forced to watch, Jay sees the thoughts of his younger self flashing like lightning bolts before his eyes.

It is at this very moment that Jay sees two lines of thoughts being formed. With one thought, Jay sees himself smiling at the young woman and telling himself that he was going to break the school's rule of no public display of affection so as to give her a soul-touching hug and deep kiss to show her his love for her. With the other thought, Jay sees himself obeying the school's rule of no public display of affection and just standing there before the young woman, telling her a simple hello before telling her that it was great to see her but that since he wasn't scheduled to be at lunch yet that he needed to get to his class before the final bell would ring.

The scene before the older Jay's eyes would then soon begin to fade back into darkness as he is once again left to his own thoughts as the shadowy hand that forced Jay to watch disappears from his face. Then, a solitary tear falls from Jay's eye as the young woman's voice tells Jay through the darkness, "What gave you the right to think that you were the only one to decide which path in life you were to take? Did your love for me not mean a single thing to you? Why didn't you just be happy and believe in what was to come afterward?".

However, before the older Jay could even give a response, he feels as though something grabs his neck from behind and is thrown backward in silence until he hears the creaking sound of a door being opened and finds Jay being thrown through the door in which he originally had been tossed through. The older Jay then falls against the hallway's wall before slumping onto the ground. Groaning, Jay moves his eyes upwards from the floor to the door as he sees it slowly closing shut before fading away as the first door did, now leaving only five doors remaining.

The old man slowly regains his composure as he gets up off of the floor. As he does, the old man sees the girl slowly changing from her child form to that of the woman she became. Once the transformation is completed, the woman tells Jay, "I told you that because you decided to alter the lifecycle the two of us were meant to be on together, and since I was forced to find my own new way, that I was serious about you being forced to face your choice. Now, I will let you continue to face those decisions and why your sanity is of your own will".

As Jay attempts to open his mouth so as to say a few words of regret, the form of Cherise fades away as silence once more returns to the dark hallway as another beam of light from winter's grasp gleams the five remaining doors in the old house's many corridors. The only sound Jay hears is that of his own heart beating and the distant sound of a clock that wasn't there before. Then, the chiming of a clock is heard as a fourth door in the hallway creaks open.

Chapter 4

The old man who calls himself Jay stands as silent as the winter's grasp on the old house as he sees yet another door slowly opening up. Frozen still, Jay wants to leave the house as he has forgotten as to why he originally entered, yet he does not as he wants to see what madness the now open door brings. As the creaking subsides and the door is now open, Jay continues to stare at the door that offers nothing more than the darkness that still swallows the house save for the light of his lantern's life. What seems like hours are only mere seconds before Jay hears a deeper set of growls emanating from the door's dark interior. Then, a set of red eyes appear from within the room.

"Oh, how you have fallen far from where you should have been," a deep voice says in between the sounds of growling. Then, the sound of something moving toward Jay is heard as the old man remains still as he sees a shadowy form walking like a beast strolls out of the door's mouth. The old man continues to stare at the shadowy creature as it slowly approaches him until it stands right before his eyes. Then, the shadow's form grows to the same height as Jay as it begins to take form. Then, the old man is now even more motionless as he is now staring at himself as though he were looking into a mirror looking back at himself.

The creature that now looks exactly like Jay stands just as motionless as the old man is standing, as it then smiles while it grows younger by a few years. "What's the matter, Jay? Don't wanna play a game with me?" the creature growls with syllables that echo exactly what the young girl Jay had seen moments earlier had spoken. "As Cherise showed you, now I remind you," the creature says as it unexpectedly places its shadowy hand upon Jay's forehead. Whereas he had forgotten with age and disease, Jay is reminded of the days, months, and years following his decision to explore the lines of the sabbatical lifecycle he found himself living.

Jay sees flashes of lightning once more cross his eyes as he sees himself in West Germany once more. Now, Jay finds himself watching his much younger self sitting at the back of a bus as it took its students home scattered across different German villages. Then, a moment arrives that sees two lines of possibilities forming invisibly above his teenage self. A moment arrives that sees him awaken to the sight of a young teenage woman talking to some other kids on the bus. The old man then sees his younger self asking a friend of his if he knew the name of the girl that he was pointing toward, to which his friend replied that her name was Mona.

A moment of recognition came to the teenage version of Jay as he knew he had arrived at another unseen fork in his life which he had known in other moments in his life. Like all the other times in his life when an important decision was to be made, Jay was unsure of what to do next after his friend had told him that she was sort of dating someone else. The old man realizes that it was at this moment that Mona was just as important to his future, to their future, but like before, Jay thought of not bothering her and remained seated in his bus seat rather than getting up to ask Mona out.

Jay's thoughts then see what he called the madness of misunderstanding the lines of possibilities that would see him wanting to touch each one. Due to not deciding to ask Mona out, the consequences then became with one girl or another being seen as different lifecycles, and each time seeing different lines of possibilities with them as well. As with each one, Jay became distracted by the other lines that were created until he could no longer recognize where he was supposed to go or who he was meant to be. Like the moment when Jay and his younger sister had asked their dad to leave the Army and West Germany, wrong decisions can just as easily become the right decisions if properly recognized in the next lifecycles. Even as Jay grew through adulthood, he would learn to better understand these lines of variations.

The lights of love passed through the old man's eyes as he saw who he had called the love of his life, Barbara, and his memories became alive once more with each beautiful year together. Then, the sight of himself losing his memories began to seep in as he witnessed his own health and sanity dwindling down with each passing day as he forgot who he was, both literally and figuratively. The natural diseases that had taken his father and his father's grandmother had combined to form something different within Jay, and what seemed like an internal madness took over.

Every decision, every possibility, whether taken or not, had a life of its own, and those lines also had the same over and over. These tidbits of information Jay once tried to tell one of his future lifecycles, Sarah but found that he could not directly tell everything which he knew. It seemed as though no matter how much Jay knew, the heavier the burden became, and the more that he could not say a single thing directly. Cherise, Jennifer, Mona, Alesa, Carlesha, Colleen, and Barbara are all that Jay remembers as the primary lines once the mainline was broken. Still, he knows there are countless others that he has never been able to remember being mapped. Jay is heartbroken from the fact that he lost his way along the way.

Then, while lost in his own thoughts, Jay is awoken once more to the sound of growling as he turns around to once more see himself standing before him. "Why show me this" the old man asks his doppelganger with tiredness now being heard in his voice. "Why not?" the lesser twin responds back, "After all, it's not anyone else's fault that the world has limped on as long as it has without help. If it wasn't for your attempts to take a sabbatical, in trying to live a normal life, then everything that is now broken would've never reached this level if you had just stuck to the plan". The old man just stands there with his head now hanging lowered, with tears flowing as his doppelganger takes the old man and leads him back to the door in which they entered.

Jay's eyes begin to dry up along with each flick, which then come back to life with each breath of life to sustain it as the light readjusts the old man's eyes to the balance of darkness and light once more. "Three doors left, Jay," a woman's voice is heard coming from behind Jay. At this point, the old man has grown more tired with each passing moment, as though winter's hold on the old house was beginning to drain him as well, so Jay turns around slowly to see who spoke. However, this time around, Jay does not see anyone.

Not a form, not a shape, just simply nothing. Then, the old man hears the same voice again coming from behind him still yet, this time saying, "How many times do you need to be reminded of who you are, why you were created, and what matters the most?". Jay turns around again. Still nothing. Then again, the same voice repeats its location from behind his back, "While we were all but still sinners, we were thrown out of Heaven for our transgressions, and our penalty for waging war was death."

Jay once again turns around, but this time says out loud, "Who are you? Show yourself!". Not a sound is heard. Jay remains motionless, half expecting one of the last three remaining doors to open up just as they have done before, but not one opens this time around. The old man's candle flickers slightly as though a breeze kissed it, and Jay knows that someone or something is now standing behind him. Jay quickly turns around, and as he does, a woman's hand grabs him by the throat, and Jay finds himself unable to either move or make the slightest sound.

As Jay looks at the woman, he quickly knows that he doesn't know who she is. The woman stands there motionless for a short time before she tilts her head to one side and to the other before speaking without moving her lips, "Show yourself? Who am I? The good questions should be who are you and know thyself!" as the woman begins to dematerialize. However, as she does, the dematerialization continues on past her hand as the old man begins to do so as well along with her until nothing remains of either of them, and darkness yet again consumes the old house.

Chapter 5

Every decision taken affects the path you take.
Every decision not taken still has a path of its own, a life
simply because it was still a possibility to take. A possible
choice, even if not actually enacted, still creates a life cycle
all its own, a choice of its own existence simply to be. The
thoughts that are Jay exist simply because he was, and is,
Jay by his mere creation alone. Even in darkness, Jay still
exists even if he cannot see himself nor the environment
around him except for his knowledge of the darkness.
Flashes of light streak across his mind's sight of everything
he recalls, does not recall, or has not yet seen in his rightful
time, illuminating the memories of life baked into the very
DNA that makes up Jay.

Even in darkness, Jay understands the importance of
simply being, even if forgotten over time. The same goes
for history. History, as it actually occurred, still exists even
if it is forgotten or attempted to be altered to fit a newer

world's understanding of its very term. Just because someone was not alive to witness something does not mean that it did not actually happen, and just because something happened does not mean that it is shared accurately. The importance of history, of time, is knowing that it exists and that the lessons of learning the truth are more important so as to learn from it and not repeat the mistakes that those who came before us did not realize that they were making at the time. The world often tells what it wants, based on who is telling the tale.

The world says to get a college education, so for those who want to get ahead, they take out loans to get a better job. However, the world pulls a cruel joke by not letting those graduate students get better-paying jobs. Promises of a better life are not fulfilled. The current world system promises shininess and fun, but not everyone sees these rewards. While many parts of the world see technological wonders, as an example, other parts remain in poverty and lack any rewards thereof.

The world sees populations with no medical help while many others have an overabundance of medical help. Those with medical access see a disproportionate of a population unable to afford medicine or have to put off medical treatment because of high costs. In fact, medical facilities and providers would either turn away patients or turn them into collection agencies rather than for them to provide any type of help.

The world sees the rich getting richer and the poor getting poorer, the homeless going with no shelter to cover them with no hope to be offered to them, and unaffordable housing is out of reach for those who were taught a dream due to landlords asking for higher than affordable prices. The way the world has been, the way it was before any of us were born, is breaking apart before our very eyes. The world cannot continue as it always has, for we now find ourselves in a broken world. A broken world that sees a majority of people with zero morality, where many do not care about anyone else but for themselves.

Even in darkness, Jay understands the importance of simply being, even if forgotten over time. Even in darkness, Jay still understands that order must still find a balance to chaos if chaos is to be controlled to a certain extent. Where once the world made sense, it now no longer does, however. Where dreams were once worth chasing after, now nightmares attack instead. Even in darkness, Jay still feels that something continues to gnaw at his soul that has been occurring for quite some time now. Even in darkness, Jay knows that this gnawing sensation has become even more relentless with time's staggering march forward.

So, even in darkness, Jay's consciousness realizes that in order for him to find the center of his world in order to find balance in it, he must always need to remember his place in the world around him, even more so when and where he forgets this detail. After all, Jay realizes that if he is to help offer the world with new ideas to help guide inspiration to its front doorstep, how can he do so if he is off-balance? So, even surrounded by darkness, Jay tells his eyelids to close so that he can ignore everything around him, the hateful world around him, for a while.

As Jay does, he can begin to see the light being emitted all around him, even through his closed eyelids. As Jay continues to keep his eyes closed, Jay begins to feel a warmth of purpose that allows him to focus better on the darkness that his soul has been traveling through. As Jay continues to keep his eyes closed, Jay's soul begins to travel back to the very beginning of everything of who Jay is and what makes up his existence, the stories that make him up with purpose.

Chapter 6

Once upon a time, there was a boy with eyes of wonder. Like other small kids, this boy soaked in the huge world around him. This boy saw the world through unfiltered eyes, recording every event and sound, photographing all with his mind.

Once upon a time, there was a boy whose parents inspired him to watch and learn from them and other family members alike. This boy's father was in the Army, so he quickly learned of his lifelong love of the military that never wavered. This boy began the love of learning from an early age and quickly adapted to new environments from that moment forward.

Once upon a time, there was a boy who, years later, had a sister born that added further value to his amazing life. Along with his newborn sister and a slightly older cousin born in the same year as the boy, more cousins would centralize the boy's life with joy.

Once upon a time, there was a boy who had a passion for history, government, geography, art, and creativity. In addition, this boy loved to listen to music, including the Baroque period of classical music and opera that coincided with museums and art galleries. Everything came together that helped shape and balance this young boy along with country music and classic rock.

Once upon a time, there was a boy who had known of the world around him, both the known and the unknown, through both curiosity and exposure that would alter this young boy's view of life. This young boy loved to learn the reasons behind things, the how's and the why's being questions often linked within his mind to what he saw all around.

This young boy saw patterns and lines of connection and eventually figured out the entire story, but this would not be the only way this young boy learned. No, this boy would also learn about God and learn from God along with all things spiritual and help drive his creative passion for writing and understanding. Of course, many of these areas occurred over the passage of time.

Once upon a time, there was a boy who started out seemingly as a normal, average little boy until one day he became very ill with a high temperature. While all seemed like he would be fine on the outside, little did anyone suspect what was going on inside this little boy's mind. For at this time, his life would either be altered dramatically or merely reawakened as the little boy found himself in a foggy forest wandering alone. Hearing a twig snap, the little boy turned his head to see a man standing before him as the man said, "Hello," before sitting down on a nearby large stone.

Once the man sat down, his hand motioned for the little boy to come over to him as though he was not a stranger. Once the little boy came over, the man picked the little boy up, sat him on his lap, and said, "Do you know who I am, Jay?". "Yes," the little boy would reply before continuing, "You're Jesus. I've always heard about you and knew of you, but was wondering about what's going on?". The man replied, "I know you're sick right now, Jay, but I wanted to come to you to remind you that you have a specific purpose in this life, and when the time comes, you will need to remember what you've lost through time so that you can piece back together everything to help fulfill your purpose." Not looking a bit surprised or confused, the little boy would reply back, "And, what's that?". "Well," Jesus would reply, "That's for you to discover, but you'll never be alone. Also, there's something I want you to know, a reminder of sorts. You once told me that you had chosen a name that would symbolize your purpose, symbolizing your gifts. So, let me remind you of this name you had chosen". Then, Jesus began to whisper into the boy's ears as his eyes opened wider.

Once these words were spoken, the little boy would soon wake up, still feeling sick and still running a fever, but would soon be back to being a little boy once more. Where once he remembered seeing things move on their own as a toddler and objects being either thrown or mists forming as an echo from when they had a solid form back in their time, the little boy would continue to see and hear things. While the unknown may frighten or intimidate others, this little boy would only be more amused with understanding. It would also take some time before this little boy would come to remember the name which the Lord had whispered into his ears.

Once upon a time, there was a boy who would grow up trying to understand everything he had seen, both with his natural eyes and the eyes of his soul. At times, this boy would find himself leaving hints for others to know that what they knew was not even the tip of the proverbial iceberg, but for the most part, he was unable to directly tell what he knew. Or, as many chess players may speculate, would not say which chess piece would be moved next so as to not tip the hand of his opponents.

Once upon a time, there was a boy with eyes of wonder. Like other small kids, this boy soaked in the huge world around him. This boy saw the world through unfiltered eyes, recording every event and sound, photographing all with his mind.

Once upon a time, there was a boy whose parents inspired him to watch and learn from them and other family members alike. This boy's father was in the Army, so he quickly learned of his lifelong love of the military that never wavered. This boy began the love of learning from an early age and quickly adapted to new environments from that moment forward.

Once upon a time, there was a boy who learned to love exploring the world around him, especially when it came to the natural world. However, the days would then draw out to a close to when he would have to go to bed and

sleep before the next day's adventures would be found.

Soon, the little boy's eyes would close to dream a little

dream, but for this small boy, his dreams would be a

message of reminder so that he would remember that he

was created for, and with, a purpose.

Chapter 7

Eyes that are closed may appear to be inactive, but many come to understand that even closed eyes are active with life, even if they are but an echo of remembrance. Even with eyes closed, other senses, such as touch and hearing, are still quite active when they are alive with life. Such is the case when the darkness within Jay's eyes fills with light as a light switch is being heard flipped on moments after a knocking is heard on a door behind him. "Yes," a woman's voice can be heard saying before finishing, "Please come in."

Jay opens his eyes as he sees that his therapist is talking with one of her coworkers, another fellow therapist, before she returns her gaze back towards him again after the other woman leaves. "So, tell me, Jay," the therapist says, "About all the doors in that darkened hallways in that old abandoned house. What do you think it symbolizes? And, why do you call this old man Jay after yourself?".

"Well, doctor," Jay starts to say before being interrupted, "Jay, I've told you before, just call me Colleen.". "Well, Colleen," Jay continues to say, "No, the old man is not myself. As you can see, I'm not old, but that's not the point. The point of the story is that the story of the old man and the hallways were all part of a series of dreams that I've had over the course of years".

Colleen, the therapist, just sits there at her desk, writing more notes down in her journal as she stares up at Jay. "Uh-huh," she would mutter in between her fingers tapping while writing with the other hand. "So you mean to tell me that everything that you told me is not about you?". "No," Jay says with a slight pause, "I mean, many of the events in between the entering and exiting of doors and the little girl are taken from parts of my life, but as I mentioned, it's not about me obviously as I'm not old." "I can see that, Jay. I'm just worried that the strains being put on your body from all the diseases and ailments that are tearing your mind and body apart are beginning to affect the core of who you are."

"Doc…er, Colleen…." Jay says before pausing as he has seemingly lost his train of thought, "I came here to speak with you about trying to understand how to balance everything out so that I can continue to keep pushing my body forward." "Well, Jay, I understand this, but you know that it's my job to make sure you are strong enough to do what you are about to do." "And, what's that, Colleen?". "That, Jay, is for you to decide while it's my job to make sure you are ready for it." The two stare at one another in awkward silence as a deep knocking noise is heard all around Jay.

"Do you hear that?" "Hear what, Jay?". Again, more knocking is heard. "That? Aren't you going to answer your door?". "Um, Jay, I don't have anyone knocking at my door." Then, a knocking is heard again, even more loudly. "Colleen," Jay says bewilderingly, "Are you telling me that you don't hear that loud knocking?". Becoming frustrated, Jay gets up from his chair and proceeds to walk over to the door before opening it.

Darkness is the only thing Jay sees when he opens the door. Then, Jay quickly looks back towards Colleen just as he sees her face becoming distorted, slowly beginning to change as though it were being flushed away until only a blank face remains. Then, out of its nostrils, a black substance begins to fall out of them and begins to swallow the body before it starts to swallow everything else up. Having no other choice but to leave the room, Jay quickly goes into the hallway of darkness. Once out, he closes the door behind him and turns back around with nothing but darkness greeting his eyes.

Eyes that are closed may appear to be inactive, but many come to understand that even closed eyes are still active with life. Even with eyes closed, other senses, such as touch and hearing, are still quite active when they are alive with life. Such is the case when the darkness within

Jay's eyes begins to fill with light as a light switch is being

heard flipped on moments after a knocking is heard on a

door behind him. "Yes," a woman's voice can be heard

saying before finishing, "Please come in."

Jay opens his eyes up to a different room engulfed

in darkness. Not sure if he is back in the old house or not,

Jay remains motionless as he allows his hearing to "see"

around him, waiting for a sign of life. Nothing can be heard

until he hears the woman's voice he had heard earlier now

saying, "I've been expecting you, Jay," as a match is struck

before it lights a candle, as a woman's figure is illuminated

as she is walking towards Jay. The world seems to change

as Jay looks down at his hands which change from an old

man's hand to a younger version as he looks up again to see

the woman now standing in front of him who reaches out

for his hand before saying, "Come with me. I want to show

you something".

As Jay walks through a hallway that seems familiar yet strangely unknown, Jay is still holding this woman's hand that is leading him down the hall, neither of them saying a word physically, yet their souls speaking volumes as though connected. Then, the woman brushes aside a curtain and takes Jay through. Then, Jay sees what looks like an old Rennaisance town come alive with him looking around from high on a villa's rooftop. Jay's ears would soon begin to hear the sounds of harps and violins being played against the backdrop of many voices that would soon see him going to the roof's edge with the woman now going down a flight of stairs alone, leaving Jay with his thoughts.

Jay quietly stands above the crowded party on the balcony overlooking a plaza below him. Everywhere he gazes, he sees people drinking and talking to one another, with a few kissing here and there. Jay places both of his arms firmly against a railing before him as though he feels the urge to seek out this woman who he had just met while trying to piece together the jumbled thoughts that take him between visions of an old man, an office, and a darkened house.

Then, Jay sees a figure partially hidden in a far corner of the plaza as his eyes begin to focus on that corner as though it were a lost soul in a sea of loneliness. Then, Jay's soul stops his mind from focusing on confusing thoughts and instead retools his mind as though his soul has found what it was searching for. Then, the figure steps out of the shadows, revealing it to be the woman who had earlier taken Jay by the hand and led him to this place. The woman knows Jay was searching for her, for she looks up to the rooftop and gives a slight smile as she then moves towards another set of smaller flights of stairs leading to an even lower part of the plaza.

To Jay, this woman's smile was as loud as a verbal yell beckoning him to come to follow her. So, Jay climbs down the flight of stairs and goes through the sea of people until he finds the set of smaller flights of stairs and heads down the path he saw the woman take. With each step taken, Jay hears the once loud ring of people's voices beginning to dim the further down the stairs he goes until silence takes over on the final step.

Looking around, Jay doesn't see anyone at first before proceeding to move forward into the center of the smaller plaza, seemingly devoid of life except his own. Jay becomes curious as to whether or not he had been mistaken about the direction this mysterious woman had gone. Perhaps she had come back up the flight of stairs as he was heading down from the rooftop and not seen her as such? As Jay turns around and begins to walk back to the flight of stairs, a noise catches his attention. "Hello?" Jay says out loud. No response. Jay then moves more towards the center of the empty plaza, illuminated on all sides by lit torches attached to the walls.

Once at the center, a noise from behind captures Jay's attention as he quickly turns around to see this woman now standing before him. "Do you know who I am?" the woman asks as Jay replies, "No. Should I?". The woman just smiles as she slowly approaches Jay while he does not move a single inch as she does. "Look into my eyes. Find the answers, and you'll know who I am". Jay finds himself unable to not look into her eyes just as she had asked, but all he sees is a reflection of himself in them as though he were looking back at himself. "You need to remember, Jay. It's important that you know who I am," the woman says to Jay before continuing to say, "And, now, you're trapped here with me" as she draws a knife seemingly from out of nowhere.

So, instead of being intimidated, Jay gives out an off-balanced quick laugh followed by a smile as the woman's once-proud smile wavers to that of a look of bewilderment. "If you don't tell me who I am, I'm going to use this knife on you until I force you to remember who I am." Jay still just stands there smiling before saying, "I'm not afraid of you or the knife. And, for the record, I'm not trapped here by you," as he gestures to the both of them.

Faster than the woman can comprehend Jay's words, she finds herself somehow disarmed as Jay quickly grabs her, spins her around, and wraps his arm around her body as he pulls her in, now holding the knife at her throat. Jay then whispers into the woman's ear, "You're trapped here with me." Shocked and confused, the woman knows she is now helpless as she screeches angrily, "Do you have a death wish?". Jay's once hostile look turns to a more calmed demeanor as he notices the tears in her now red-rimmed eyes as they fall to the cobble-stoned floor below.

Now, Jay becomes confused as he drops the knife and turns the woman back around to face him as he says, "I'm confused. I don't" – "Stop," the woman says as she cuts Jay's words, "just stop.". The woman's anger, the look of bitterness, was now gone as she slumped to the ground, exhausted. The woman then takes a deep echoing breath. Jay's mouth does not say a single word, but his eyes tell all as Jay kneels to the ground and slowly embraces the woman's body in his arms, pulling her tightly to his body.

Then, the sound of a single pair of clapping hands is heard behind the two of them as they instinctively look together simultaneously. "Bravo, bravo!" says a man as he steps out from the shadows. "Quite the show! But now I'm curious. What happens next? Do the two of you really know what's truly going on?" the man says as his face slightly changes in appearance the closer he walks towards Jay and the unnamed woman.

"You," the woman whispers out as Jay looks at her and asks, "You know him?", as the stranger then says in response, "It's the same question this young lady asked you, Jay, just as I'm now telling you. Tell me who this woman is and tell me who I am". Then, another voice comes out asking the same as another man appears and then another and then another until there are now a total of six people now on the small plaza. As Jay looks all around him, the woman that was just at his mercy now gets up and stands even closer to him as though she is now frightened. "Jay," the woman whispers, "Now would be a very good time for you to remember," as each person's face is continuously being distorted by both the light of the torches and the shadows of the night.

"I have no idea who any of you are," Jay says out loud. "Then, let me take the opportunity to introduce each other to you one by one, all seven gathered here at this very moment. Over there, the young boy is you, when you were but a wee lad. The other one over there is who we call the historian and the librarian, the creative one who also is a minister. That man over there, he's who we call the tech and scientific one, but he's more of a crueler version of you in that he has no time for waste. And, you've already met the young woman, along with me, who I would describe as the tactician, the politician if you will. Then, there's you."

Jay cannot find any words to speak as he looks at each of them, even more so at the woman who now reapproaches Jay.

"You, Jay," the woman whispers, "need to remember who you are, who we all are, so that we can move forward. Without you, we are nothing, and we are lost. You're the host, the main point among so many lines of the existence of possibilities, and we are all those possibilities. We are all different, yet we are the same". "Wait a minute," Jay whispers back to her, "That person, the tactician, said there were seven, but he only named six…" before being interrupted by the main speaker, "Ah, the seventh" he says before giving a quick chuckle. "The seventh one, well, he's all around us, the shadows that tie our bloodlines together from the very beginning."

Before Jay can even utter another syllable, the woman places a note in his hand before saying, "Jay, you don't have much time left. Your body is already beginning to fail you, and we all need you to remember your purpose in the world". As Jay looks down to open the note, he looks back up real quick to ask the woman another question, but he sees that she is gone when he does. In fact, all of the others are gone. Then, Jay looks back down at the note, opening it as he attempts to wrap his mind around everything that is going on. Then, Jay reads the note which says, "Faith is the foundation of your existence. Remember the words of Jesus. Face the shadow, face yourself, so that you walk according to plan and purpose. You have but only a short time before the end".

Then, Jay begins to see his hands turn once more to those of an old man's, as he has been used to for quite some time now. Jay drops the paper as it disappears as though it were never really there, to begin with. Then, Jay hears a hissing sound emanating from the shadows themselves.

Becoming curious, Jay walks slowly towards the shadows,

but the hissing dies down in tone with each step he takes.

As Jay finally nears the edge of the shadows, a voice that

taunted him in the house that started this insanity whispers

to him, "Let's play the final game, shall we?" as a shadowy

arm reaches out and pulls Jay into the darkness. It is in the

darkness that Jay realizes he must keep his eyes closed so

as to remember who he is and where he has come from if

he is to survive what is to come. So, with beams of

Heavenly light, Jay remembers.

Chapter 8

123 generations. This is the number from which begins my story with my existence being in mind from God. From here, God created Adam before creating Eve through Adam's rib, from whom we all share common ties as a unified human race. My story then continues through Seth, Enosh, Kenan, Mahalalel, Jared, Enoch, Methuselah, Lamech, and then to Noah, with whom all of us also share ties with.

My story then differs from some of you as my beginnings then continued on through Shem, Arphaxad, Cainan, Shelah, Eber, Peleg, Reu, Serug, Nahor, Terah, and then to Abram before God had changed his name to Abraham, as recorded in both the Torah and the Bible. Through Abraham, my story continues on to Isaac, Jacob, Judah, Perez, Hezron, Arni, Admin, Amminadab, Nahshon, Salmon, Boaz, Obed, and Jesse continue my Jewish heritage and my being a part of one of the Twelve Tribes of

Judah, the tribe of Judah itself. From Jesse, as both the Torah and the Bible record, came my 88th great-grandfather, King David, and through him and Bathsheba came two of 87th great-grandfathers whose lines both divide and unite my existence, King Soloman and his brother Nathan. The Torah and the Bible chronicle the rest of these two branches of what I have seen on my family tree as the central roots around which all my other bloodlines flow.

Both Holy Texts do not show what happens to my Jewish bloodlines following the siege of Jerusalem by the Romans a few years not long after the martyrdom of James. In the year 70 A.D., the Roman Empire laid siege to both the Holy City of Jerusalem and the Second Holy Temple that saw many of my Jewish family and brethren whisked away to other parts of the region, Asia, and Europe, and a large branch of my bloodline becoming Exilarchs in Persian Mesopotamia. From there, my Jewish origins made more of a presence in later centuries on the Eastern European continent then on to the rest of Europe. For meaning in the modern world, I am of Ashkenazi Jewish descent, as my DNA reflects, and of which are the two central branches of all my other essential bloodlines.

While my Davidian Jewish bloodlines are the two central branches of my existence, they are not the only major bloodlines that flow through my veins and within my DNA. No, you see, I have only accounted for at least close to 5000 individuals who contributed to helping ensure I came to be with a specific purpose in mind through God's grand design for my life, and I am sure there are many more yet to discover. Now, here are just some of the examples that cover the thousands of individuals that have lived so that I could live as well and to share life with in no particular order except listed in specific sections of mind:

- President Bill Clinton (7th cousin 1x removed)

- President Theodore Roosevelt (5th cousin 5x removed)

- President George Washington (1st cousin 9x removed)

- President Harry S. Truman (6th cousin 6x removed)

- First Lady Michelle Obama (8th cousin 2x removed)

- President Zachary Taylor (4th cousin 7x removed)

- President Abraham Lincoln (5th cousin 5x removed)

- President George H.W. Bush (7th cousin 1x removed)

- President George W. Bush (8th cousin)

- President Thomas Jefferson (4th cousin 8x removed)

- President Joe Biden (8th cousin 2x removed)

- President Jimmy Carter (7th cousin 4x removed)

- President Franklin Pierce (5th cousin 6x removed)

- Vice President George Clinton (4th cousin 8x removed)

- President Lyndon B. Johnson (6th cousin 4x removed)

- President John F. Kennedy (7th cousin 4x removed)

- President Richard Nixon (7th cousin 3x removed)

- President Calvin Coolidge (7th cousin 4x removed)

- Vice President Charles Curtis (7th cousin 3x removed)

- President James Madison (3rd cousin 9x removed)

- President Ronald Reagan (7th cousin 4x removed)

- President John Adams (4th cousin 8x removed)

- First Lady, Senator & Secretary Hilary Clinton (8th cousin 1x removed)

- President Dwight D. Eisenhower (6th cousin 5x removed)

- President John Quincy Adams (5th cousin 8x removed)

- President James Buchanan (3rd cousin 6x removed)

- President Andrew Jackson (4th cousin 7x removed)

- President Millard Fillmore (5th cousin 6x removed)

- President Franklin Delano Roosevelt (5th cousin 5x removed)

- First Lady Eleanor Roosevelt (6th cousin 4x removed)

- First Lady Margaret Mackall Taylor (4th cousin 7x removed)

- Vice President John Nance Garner (7th cousin 4x removed)

- President Donald Trump (7th cousin 4x removed)

- Vice President Mike Pence (8th cousin)

- Vice President Barack Obama (7th cousin 1x removed)

- Vice President Dick Cheney (8th cousin 1x removed)

- President James Monroe (9th cousin)

- Vice President Aaron Burr (1st cousin 8x removed)

- General & Secretary Colin Powell (7th cousin 3x removed)

- Thomas Paine (6th cousin x removed)

- Speaker of the House Newt Gingrich (6th cousin 3x removed)

- Benjamin Franklin (2nd cousin 9x removed)

- Senator & Secretary John Kerry (8th cousin 2x removed)

- Governor & Senator Mitt Romney (7th cousin 1x removed)

- Miles Davis (7th cousin 2x removed)

- Jackie Robinson (8th cousin 2x removed)

- Beyonce (8th cousin 1x removed)

- Jesse Owens (7th cousin 4x removed)

- Halle Berry (8th cousin 1x removed)

- Kanye West (8th cousin 2x removed)

- Otis Redding (9th cousin)

- Cab Calloway (8th cousin 2x removed)

- George Washington Carver (6th cousin 6x removed)

- Harriet Tubman (6th cousin 5x removed)

- Alex Haley (6th cousin 4x removed)

- Nat "King" Cole (7th cousin 3x removed)

- Al Sharpton (7th cousin 3x removed)

- Denzel Washington (8th cousin)

- Martin Luther King Jr (8th cousin 2x removed)

- Quincy Jones (6th cousin 4x removed)

- Malcolm X (6th cousin 4x removed)

- Jimi Hendrix (7th cousin 2x removed)

- Michael Jackson (8th cousin 2x removed)

- Jon Huntsman (8th cousin)

- Josh Brolin (8th cousin 1x removed)

- James Cagney (6th cousin 3x removed)

- Cecile B DeMille (8th cousin 2x removed)

- Matthew McConaughey (7th cousin 2x removed)

- Joe Louis (8th cousin)

- Don Henley (5th cousin 3x removed)

- Rosa Parks (7th cousin 3x removed)

- John Wesley (2nd cousin 11x removed)

- David Cameron (8th cousin 2x removed)

- Wolfgang Amadeus Mozart (5th cousin 8x removed)

- Johann Sebastian Bach (3rd cousin 10x removed)

- Stevie Nicks (8th cousin 1x removed)

- George Harrison (8th cousin 2x removed)

- Avril Lavigne (9th cousin)

- Sir Winston Churchill (6th cousin 2x removed)

- Demi Lovato (8th cousin 1x removed)

- Stephen Amell (8th cousin)

- Kevin Bacon (8th cousin 2x removed)

- Thomas Edison (6th cousin 5x removed)

- Warren Buffet (9th cousin)

- Stephen F. Austin (6th cousin 5x removed)

- Tim Burton (8th cousin 1x removed)

- Miley Cyrus (8th cousin 1x removed)

- Bill Gates (8th cousin)

- Walt Disney (7th cousin 3x removed)

- Cate Blanchett (6th cousin 2x removed)

- Luke Bryan (9th cousin)

- Carrie Underwood (9th cousin)

- Jessica Simpson (7th cousin 2x removed)

- Carrie Fisher (9th cousin)

- Blake Shelton (6th cousin 2x removed)

- Helen Keller (7th cousin 4x removed)

- Johnny Cash (7th cousin 2x removed)

- Brad Paisley (8th cousin 1x removed)

- Eminem (9th cousin)

- Willie Nelson (7th cousin 1x removed)

- Ron Howard (8th cousin 1x removed)

- Reese Witherspoon (8th cousin 1x removed)

- Johnny Depp (7th cousin 1x removed)

- Audrey Hepburn (7th cousin 3x removed)

- Grace Kelly (8th cousin 2x removed)

- Shania Twain (9th cousin)

- Julia Roberts (8th cousin 2x removed)

- General Robert E. Lee (4th cousin 7x removed)

- Henry David Thoreau (6th cousin 5x removed)

- Mark Twain (5th cousin 3x removed)

- Edgar Allan Poe (4th cousin 6x removed)

- E.E. Cummings (6th cousin 4x removed)

- Jane Austen (5th cousin 8x removed)

- Stephen King (7th cousin 2x removed)

- Walt Whitman (5th cousin 5x removed)

- Jack London (7th cousin 2x removed)

- Lewis Carroll (6th cousin 6x removed)

- William Blake (5th cousin 7x removed)

- Alex Haley (6th cousin 4x removed)

- Emily Dickinson (5th cousin 5x removed)

- John Steinbeck (7th cousin 4x removed)

- Margaret Atwood (6th cousin 1x removed)

- Agatha Christie (8th cousin 2x removed)

- Sir Walter Scott (3rd cousin 8x removed)

- Ernest Hemingway (8th cousin 2x removed)

- A.A. Milne (7th cousin 4x removed)

- Pearl S. Buck (4th cousin 5x removed)

- Robert Louis Stevenson (6th cousin 5x removed)

- F. Scott Fitzgerald (6th cousin 4x removed)

- Henry Miller (2nd cousin 8x removed)

- Beatrix Potter (7th cousin 4x removed)

- Emily Post (5th cousin 5x removed)

- Oscar Wilde (6th cousin 5x removed)

- Virginia Woolf (7th cousin 4x removed)

- Thomas Hardy (7th cousin 4x removed)

- George Eliot (4th cousin 7x removed)

- William Butler Yeats (7th cousin 4x removed)

- Stephanie Meyer (8th cousin 1x removed)

- Bram Stoker (6th cousin 6x removed)

- Rudyard Kipling (6th cousin 6x removed)

- George Orwell (7th cousin 3x removed)

- William Wordsworth (4th cousin 8x removed)

- Alfred Tennyson (5th cousin 7x removed)

- Truman Capote (8th cousin 2x removed)

- Plantagenet dynasty

- Stuart dynasty

- Tudor dynasty

- Capetian dynasty

- Carolingian dynasty

- Merovingian dynasty

Some of my other more notable ancestors include:

- King Seleucus I Nicator of Babylon, Mesopotamia, and Persia (founder of Seleucid Empire) (76th great-grandfather)

- Alexander the Great (81st great-grandfather)

- King Clovis I (48th great grandfather)

- King Pepin the Short (38th great grandfather)

- Emperor Charlemagne (37th great grandfather)

- King Hugh Capet (35th great grandfather)

- King Robert I, also known as King Robert the
Bruce (34th great-grandfather)

- William the Conqueror (27th great-grandfather)

- King Henry VIII (16th great-grandfather)

- Emperor Ferdinand I of Austria (6th cousin 6x
removed)

- King Charles I (10th great-granduncle)

- King James VI of Scotland (11th great-grandfather)

- Queen Mary I of Scots (12th great-grandmother)

- Hedwig Duchess of Bavaria (37th great-
grandmother)

- King Njord of the Swedes (62nd great-grandfather)

- King Yngvi-Freyr I of Sweden (Uppsala dynasty -
50th great-grandfather)

- King Harald I Haraldsson of Norway (41st great-
grandfather)

- King Benard I of Italy (36th great-grandfather)

- Sir Walter Raleigh (14th great-grandfather)

As given the few examples are given and many not given (I also have great-grandfathers who were chieftains in Ireland, including County Cavan, Dublin, and other areas), I share the bloodlines of all the modern European monarchs past and present with my DNA giving evidence of sharing other royalties with those of the Romanovs and Windsors.

While I share either direct or indirect bloodlines with American, European, Middle Eastern, African, and Jewish history (my DNA reflects Ashkenazi Jewish, Finnish, Native American, French/German, and Northwestern European ties), I also have links to the Persian Empire, ancient Egypt, and others with short sample examples including:

- King Darius the Great or Darius I (Achaemenid Empire) (81st great-grandfather)

- King Xerxes I (Achaemenid Empire) (80th great-grandfather)

- King Artaxerxes I of Persia (Achaemenid Empire) (79th great-grandfather)

- Ptolemaic Dynasty of Egypt (including Pharoah Ptolemy I of Egypt and Cleopatra)

My additional ancestral ties include the Viking Danish, the Icelandic Vikings, the Celts, the Franks, the Britons, Celtic Britons, Celtic Brigantes, Celtic Cantiaci, Celtic Parisi, the Saxons, the Picts, the Longobards, the Celtic Dobunni, the Vandals, the Swedish Vikings, the Scythians, the Ostrogoths, and the Belgae.

My more recent direct ancestry line of Raley found themselves being smuggled to the new world aboard the English ships, the Ark and the Dove, on March 23, 1634, after having left the Isle of Wight on November 22, 1633. Due to the constant wars and killings between the Catholics and the Protestants, especially between many of my shared/common family members and royal family members, they needed to be smuggled away in the hope of starting a life free of persecution. My Raley family members helped found the first Catholic colony in the English new world in what they named St. Mary's in Maryland the same year they landed in 1634. Due to the nature of privacy for many of those who and I share the same last name, I can at least say that I have a family full of service members and loving members who have all contributed to who I am today. Especially for all those who came before me and the thousands whose blood still runs through my existence today.

I am a shadow within the shadow of history whose family members stayed below the gaze of time's understanding. My name has been known only by those whose lives crossed mine, whether it is personally, academically, or professionally. My published works reflect dreams being realized yet not yet marketed to the general population. Recent technological sightings give the world a glimpse of who I seem to be, but I remain nothing more than a quick internet search by differing names to the world at large. My ideas and thoughts have been shared with many, some known with many anonymously unknown. While history records many of my various family members' lives throughout its conception, I have only occasionally peeked past its veil before once more remaining within history's shadows. Until now.

Chapter 9

Darkness. An echoing knock on a wooden door repeats three times the same. Silence. Three more times, an echoing knock on a wooden door repeats in the same manner. Silence. An echoing knock on a wooden door begins its third repetitive start, only to be interrupted after the next first try when the creaking sound of the wooden door is heard before the second knock can be made. Then, silence once more. That is until footsteps can be heard shuffling through the darkness and the creaking sound of a wooden door being closed.

Then, the sound of a match being struck against its home is heard as the faint glow of the match's reason for existing slowly brightens to full life. The match then moves through the air as though it were dancing a lonesome, slow Walz, being mindful of each step it takes in tune with the sound of unsee shuffling fee. The match's slow dance continues on for a bit more until it remains still before it rises as though it were about to give a toast to its once meaningful life. Then, the outline of a lantern is seen with a candle inside as the match lays down its life so that the candle can begin its own, and the lantern's latch is closed so as to protect it.

The lantern then is carefully raised until the face of an older man is seen trying to make the acquaintance between the darkness, his eyes, and the candle's light. The old man begins to slowly walk forward through the darkness before him, occasionally looking down toward his feet as though the candlelight was telling him to be careful with each step. Through the mixture of the light's shadows gently nudging away the darknesses' hold, the older man takes note of the room he's now standing in.

Looking around, the man sees a room in shambles, old pieces of furniture covered in blankets of dust with old books and unseen faces of pictures littering an old wooden floor as though it were part of a snowglobe shaken up.

Winter's breath grees the man's life as he lifts the lantern a little higher until the squint of his eye reveals what he wants to see as he begins to talk a bit furthermore. The old man is now standing before what appears to be a long hallway, and as his eyes adjust, he sees the outline of two doorways on each side of the corridor that has an ever more darkened end.

Then, an unseen voice calls out, "Well, aren't you going to open one of them up?". "No. Not this time," the old man responds. "I'm going to tell you right now that it's time you started to play my game. I'm not running, I'm not going to hide, and I'm definitely not going to open one of these doors. I have a purpose, so it's time you came to me so that we can finish this dance." Then, one of the two doors slowly creaks open. A familiar little girl then appears next to the old man as she asks, "So, you remember now?". "Yes, Cherise," replies the old man as he continues, "it is definitely time now" as the old man then refocuses his attention to the opened door.

Then, five familiar faces step out as they all merge into one single ball of light that enters the old man and begins to transform him into a less old version of himself. Jay then briefly opens his eyes to see a shadowy trail seeping from the still opened door as Jay once more closes his eyes and knows what is about to happen. With his eyes still shut, Jay tells Cherise, "Yes, I do remember."

123 generations. This is the number from which begins my story with my existence being in mind from God. My story differs from many of you as I have seen the many lines of possibilities alongside the lives I have lived and the lives I could have lived. As the world begins to crumble all around, all I can think about is my purpose, what I was designed to do. The world's problems cannot be solved with old ways of thinking. The world's problems cannot be solved with rehashed ideas. No, it's time that I

stepped out from the shadows and carefully helped maneuver this common world to where it needs to be so that a new tomorrow can finally begin.

A new system for a new world, a path that will finally end all of this madness once and for all. So, now I say my chosen name as it was once attributed to an old Celtic legend where the ability to speak to others so as to help them see the way in which to travel was given. I know that I have a short time to accomplish what I can, but the world needs to hear new words and ideas for new solutions. Let my words go forth as paths before my story ends. I am Ogmios, and this is how my story begins.